CW01082250

FIRST STORY

First Story changes lives through writing.

We believe that writing can transform lives, and that there is dignity and power in every young person's story.

First Story brings talented, professional writers into secondary schools serving low-income communities to work with teachers and students to foster creativity and communication skills. By helping students find their voices through intensive, fun programmes, First Story raises aspirations and gives students the skills and confidence to achieve them.

For more information and details of how to support First Story, see www.firststory.org.uk or contact us at info@firststory.org.uk.

A Thousand Stories Under a Lid
ISBN 978-0-85748-184-9

Published by First Story Limited
www.firststory.org.uk
Sixth Floor
2 Seething Lane
London
EC3N 4AT

Copyright © First Story 2015

Typesetting: Avon DataSet Ltd
Cover Design: Brett Biedscheid
Printed in the UK by Intype Libra Ltd

First Story is a registered charity number 1122939 and a private company limited by guarantee
incorporated in England with number 06487410. First Story is a business name of First Story Limited.

A Thousand Stories Under a Lid

An Anthology

BY THE FIRST STORY GROUP
AT BRADFORD ACADEMY

EDITED AND INTRODUCED BY STAN SKINNY | 2015

FIRST STORY
Creativity Literacy Confidence

As Patron of First Story I am delighted that it continues to foster and inspire the creativity and talent of young people in challenging secondary schools.

I firmly believe that nurturing a passion for reading and writing is vital to the health of our country. I am therefore greatly encouraged to know that young people in this school – and across the country – have been meeting each week throughout the year in order to write together.

I send my warmest congratulations to everybody who is published in this anthology.

HRH The Duchess of Cornwall

Thank You

Melanie Curtis at **Avon DataSet** for her overwhelming support for First Story and for giving her time in typesetting this anthology.

Brett Biedscheid for designing the cover of this anthology.

Intype Libra for printing this anthology at a discounted rate, **Tony Chapman** and **Moya Birchall** at Intype Libra for their advice.

Arts Council England which supported First Story in this school.

HRH The Duchess of Cornwall, Patron of First Story.

The Trustees of First Story:
Ed Baden-Powell, Beth Colocci, Sophie Dalling, Charlotte Hogg, Sue Horner, Rob Ind, Andrea Minton Beddoes, John Rendel, Alastair Ruxton, Mayowa Sofekun, David Stephens and Betsy Tobin.

The Advisory Board of First Story:
Andrew Adonis, Julian Barnes, Jamie Byng, Alex Clark, Julia Cleverdon, Andrew Cowan, Jonathan Dimbleby, Mark Haddon, Simon Jenkins, Derek Johns, Andrew Kidd, Rona Kiley, Chris Patten, Kevin Prunty, Zadie Smith, William Waldegrave and Brett Wigdortz.

Thanks to:
Arts Council England, Authors' Licensing and Collecting Society, Jane and Peter Aitken, Tim Bevan and Amy Gadney, Suzanne Brais and Stefan Green, Boots Charitable Trust, the Boutell Bequest, Clifford Chance Foundation, Clore Duffield Foundation, Beth and Michele Colocci, the Danego Charitable Trust, the Dulverton Trust, the Drue Heinz Trust, Edwin Fox Foundation, Gerald Fox, Esmée Fairbairn Foundation, the Thomas Farr Charity, the First Story Events Committee, the First Story First Editions Club,

the Robert Gavron Charitable Trust, the Girdlers' Company Charitable Trust, Give a Book, the Golden Bottle Trust, Goldman Sachs Gives, the Goldsmiths' Company Charity, Kate Harris, the Laura Kinsella Foundation, Kate Kunac-Tabinor, the Lake House Charitable Foundation, John Lyon's Charity, Sir George Martin Trust, Mercers' Company Charitable Foundation, Michael Morpurgo, Old Possum's Practical Trust, Oxford University Press, Philip Pullman, the Pitt Rivers Museum, Psycle Interactive, Laurel and John Rafter, the Sigrid Rausing Trust, Clare Reihill, the Royal Society of Literature, Santander, Neil and Alison Seaton, the Staples Trust, Teach First, the Francis Terry Foundation, Betsy Tobin and Peter Sands, the Trusthouse Charitable Foundation, University College Oxford, Garfield Weston Foundation, Caroline and William Waldegrave, and Walker Books.

Most importantly we would like to thank the students, teachers and writers who have worked so hard to make First Story a success this year, as well as the many individuals and organisations (including those who we may have omitted to name) who have given their generous time, support and advice.

Contents

Introduction

Stan Skinny

WRITER-IN-RESIDENCE

'Ku Na Ha, Ku Na Ha,' I asked the group to blast out, hopping from foot to foot in the traditional sun dance while worried librarians looked on. They need not have worried – we were merely unleashing our inner creative beings, or beenings, and to my glee the group happily obliged.

Throughout this last year I've got to know this wonderful group of open-minded and creative young people who aren't scared to try out unusual things and go to unusual places in their imaginations – and gone we have. In this collection you will find stories and poems of flowerpots, aquaragyms, heavenly train journeys, guinea pigs, frozen moms and talking ukuleles, and it's been a blast being at the inception of these marvellous worlds.

It's titled *A Thousand Stories Under a Lid* and I feel this aptly describes many people's creativity: that we contain it under a lid and put it on the shelf, safely tucked away.

Fortunately, through the fantastic First Story programme, we've had an opportunity to unleash our creative beasts, flinging our lids far into the distance. And inside we find there are thousands – millions, even – of words desperate to get out.

As Lydia, one of our writers, puts it, 'under my lid you will find a spring coiled up, ready to bounce'. Our creativity is like a wound spring desperate to come out, and after reading this I hope you too are encouraged to open your creative lid, because creativity is what makes us human. It's what gave us the idea to walk on two legs, to invent things, to find solutions to problems, to entertain, encourage and enlighten.

There are stories in everyone. It has been wonderful to be part of this process, to be part of First Story, and to hear the many stories from the students of Bradford Academy.

I wish to thank all the students for their enthusiasm and talent, and I hope they continue to write (and write about) their lives. Also this project would have not been possible without the enormous efforts of Kayleigh Marsden and Alexandra Homayoonpoor whose assistance and support in class has been invaluable.

Enjoy, and remember, if you ever get stuck, *Ku Na HA*.

A Group Poem

Under My Lid You Will Find

Under my lid you will find:
A spring coiled up, ready to bounce
A calculator that has forgotten how to count
A spun spiderweb but no spider
A lock of Bigfoot's fur
and a Hadron collider

You will find
My brother's old glasses with the smashed right lens
A handkerchief covered in dirt
And the empty pots of Bill and Ben

You will find
A sponge (my brain) so saturated it overflows
My secret life that even I don't know
An unknown story from long ago

You'll find who I love
And who I hate with a vengeance
And a golden gleaming pendant

You will find a stash of gleaming stolen cash
A mountain of detention slips
And a big bowl of mash

You will find
A dinosaur, which rampages and roars
A colony of fishes swimming away from spear-shaped sharks
and a sea full of stars

And when you find there is no hope,
in that cruel dark universe
you will find a voice
a creative spark
under my lid.

Mohammad Talha Ahmed

I Am Talha

I am Talha.
I am beautiful and bronze
my body is skinny and my head is flat
I have been put in a box and mailed down the stairs
I like to shower
and keep myself clean
and have taught my cat
how to groom

Inspire Me

Before I'm old and cold
Before I'm no longer bold
Before we meet the last tide
Inspire me tonight

For my youth
For my generations
To be a leader
To save the last of us

Inspire me to write
Inspire me to create
Inspire me to speak
Inspire me to inspire others too

Before the wind blows no more
Before the stars shine no more
Before nothing makes us smile
Inspire me for a while

For the kids
For the lost ones
To be a leader
To save the last of us
inspire me

Bridges

I am beauty and the beast
Above and below
I arise and descend
With the traffic flow
I can arch or I can be flat

You need me
I am your unsung knight
You like to look at me sometimes
I can make the city bright

I am the way over the water
depended upon
I am the messiah
the way along
I have the strength of Hercules

Choose Your Own Adventure

Self disappointment wasn't enough,
To them disappointing
Demoralising context & horrid
Nature. Obsessive little child
Lost in wanting to be lost.
'Escape me, oh dear escapism.'
Quotes self to quote no one.
Choose your own adventure.
Fascinating, scintillating
Bigger & brighter future now.
Go to university, get a job.
Escape me not my passions
Curate but can't cure it
Rain on my reign.
Choose your own adventure
What life do you want to live?
What story do you want to tell?
Self loathing. Self loving.
All grown but didn't grow up
Past present collide
Painstaking present or failing future.
Escapism was my adventure.

Daniaal Mahmood

The Watering Can

As I stared at the watering can, pale blue water trickled down from its green body. As it gleamed from the sun's rays I remembered a show that used to make me smile. *Bill and Ben the Flowerpot Men*. When I was a young child I could not eat my breakfast without watching this show. It was an addiction that could not be suppressed. It went as far as me wearing the costumes the characters wore. A brown pot for a cap, a flimsy red-faced mask with a great big plant pot around my midriff and tight green pants.

I marched into the garden with Bill and Ben hanging from the rims of my pocket. This is where the adventure became a reality...

Day by day, playtime would get longer, Ben and Bill at my side as the sun would rise and fall on hot summer days. Every day was a new adventure; a day fighting off the tomato army, a day taming the great water hose or a day at the sprinklers where it showered galore. I decided to make the two friends into three, and I became Bob. So, now it was the three amigos: Bob, Ben and Bill.

As time passed, I knew I would have to grow up. I was getting older and the programme that used to air every morning before I went to school was now a vague memory. My interest had gone, and along with it so did my childish dreams.

Staring at the bare green watering can, I wondered to myself,

'Will I ever be a child again, the same happy chappy who would trot round his garden with a smile across his face?' But then those childish dreams of mine began to flow back into my mind, and I thought, 'why not?' For one last time I picked up the watering can and pottered down the garden, embarking on one last adventure with Bill and Ben.

Golden Sand

Droplets of blood trickled through the thick golden sand and bled into the vast ocean. Slowly it turned, mutated from calm blue to rigorous red. This was no beach for the drunk and merry: it was a beach for the dead, the fallen, and the heroes.

Acres of land had been bombarded with many strong attacks, humungous craters etched into the silent landscape. No signs of life; had life lost its fight?

No movement could I see, no sound could I hear, only the sounds of blood dripping from the corpses grasping at the sharp, shipwrecked edge. Everywhere I turned, bodies accompanied me, scattered everywhere.

The deceased lay rotting, giving off a hideous stench that poisoned the air. No birds could be seen, all lost, hiding in the dark clouds hovering over me. How many more enemies still lurked behind the walls?

As my friends lay dead, the sunshine seeped through the cracks of the sky, illuminating the space around me, and reminded me of the days where my family and I would take long strolls along the beach shore. A bright sunny day was all that we needed to pack our bags and leave for the beach. I remember how excited I would become when it came to lunchtime, as I raced off to the fish and chip store with my drool creating endless pools of water. Most importantly, I clung on to the memory of my time with my family before the struggles that now bound me here to die.

Lost deep in my thoughts, the battle commenced. The sound of agony began to scar my brain. Was I the only survivor? Me, trying to live until help arrived. How could I survive through this? My supplies were low but I leapt into the enemy's territory with all guns blazing. Each bullet of mine punctured those who

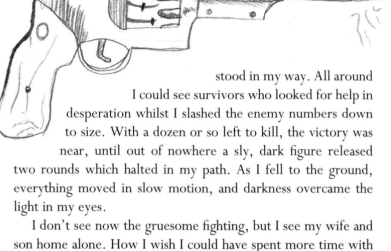

stood in my way. All around I could see survivors who looked for help in desperation whilst I slashed the enemy numbers down to size. With a dozen or so left to kill, the victory was near, until out of nowhere a sly, dark figure released two rounds which halted in my path. As I fell to the ground, everything moved in slow motion, and darkness overcame the light in my eyes.

I don't see now the gruesome fighting, but I see my wife and son home alone. How I wish I could have spent more time with them but fate decided my end. *Click click click*

Samiual Mahmood

Remembrance Sunday

In a field of flowers,
Lies a fleet of bright red poppies,
So many, they look photocopied.

I Am Fish

I am fish
fish fish fish,
my name
it echoes throughout the land
I am
the fastest
most intelligent
of all fish
others have met the vinegar
been dipped in tomato
have sat next to the chip
but not me
I swim through
all obstacles ahead

they call me fearless
they call me powerful
they call me superstitious

they call me Fish.

The Trip

I remember
The wavy hard sand,
Warming my feet,
in a place
Called Santander.
It wasn't the same
The next time around
The endless miles of golden sand,
replaced by an army of carpet
The walls covered in red berry blast paint.
Whilst having a wonderful time,
I knew it had come to an end.
it would be the last time
I go on a bank holiday.

Burger Bun

Bennie bit the burger bun,
The burger bun bit Bennie,
Bennie bit it back again –
It only cost a penny.

Seren Robb

Seren

My name is Seren
It means star
In a tongue that is not my own

My name consists only of a sentence
Whilst others' are a full page

If I was an Alice, Mary, or Jane

I would have had
several paragraphs
Recounting the proud heritage of the word

Alice is noble, a child of the heather
Mary is wished for, holy and bitter
Jane is gracious and merciful

Whilst my name has only one meaning
One thing to strive for

There are a billion stars in the sky
Insignificant

Yet stars tell stories,
Forgotten tales,
Like the hunter killed by Artemis,
The scorpion lit by fire,
The queen tossed through space.

I can't imagine being parted from my name.
If I had I been an Alice, Mary or Jane
I would not be the same person I am today.

My name is Seren,
It only has one meaning.

The rest of the page I will just write myself.

Fair Lintilla

Fair Lintilla,
Queen of the fairies,
Her beauty is matched by one only,
Who dwells behind glass.
The only one she'll leave be.

Fair Lintilla,
A pure white rose,
Behind red lips she hides her thorns.
Within the garden in which she blooms,
The other flowers' heads are pruned.

Fair Lintilla
Casts her gaze
Towards the realm of man.
So many items she desires,
So many playthings she shall have.

Fair Lintilla
Tricks young men,
Tempts them with her riches,
Till they fall, then resistance ceases.
They are hers forever.

Fair Lintilla
Sends out her folk in the dead of night,
Through Mother windows they then climb.
When the poor maid awakes she finds the cradle to be bare!
Or worse, something else is hidden there.

Fair Lintilla,
The fairy queen,
Has the pretty ones brought to her.
Then she takes them up into her arms,
And in one gulp consumes them!

Fair Lintilla,
Her lips are lust,
Her eyes are greed and envy.
Within the mirror lies her only love,
She will never part their company.

When Lintilla's winter comes.
When red petals wither and fall.
Only then can the people rejoice.

Only to witness
the next flowers
    bloom.

A Poem Based on the Works of Edward Gorey

A is for Alex who drowned in a lake.
B is for Beth, baked into a cake.

C is for Craig, lost in a storm.
D is for Dora, hung and drawn.

E is for Emma who left with a bang.
F for Flora, left there to hang.

G is for George, left out in the cold.
H is for Henry whose organs were sold.

I is for Isaac, run down by a train,
And also Immanuel, whose fate was the same.

J is for Jessica who left naught but ash.
L is for Luke in an unfortunate crash.

M is for Mike who dug his own grave.
N is for Nigel, dragged in a bear's cave.

O is for Otto at whom the crows peck.
P is for Pippa in a shipwreck.

Q is for Quentin who thought he could fly.
R is for Rachel, shot in the eye.

S is for Simon who sank in a bog.
T is for Tabitha, ravaged by dogs.

U is for Umerus, by book and bell.
V is for Vincent so he never would tell.

W is for William who was coughing up blood.
X is for Xander, lost alone in the wood.

Y is for Yvette who was on the wrong side.
Z is for Zephaniah no one cares how he died.

K is for Kate, who the poet forgot,
But like all the others she surely will rot.

Catherine on the Train

Condensation had formed around the edges of the window. Catherine watched as her hands changed colour beneath the orange street lights that shone through. She could hear the train's breath as it continued to move, clattering against the tracks. In her hands she clutched a slip of paper. A distant whistle sounded as the train slowed, reaching a station. The platform was small with a few small bushes decorating the edge. Catherine was shocked at the number of people she saw waiting there. They all stood in a clump together; it reminded her of something she had seen in a nature documentary once of how penguins flocked together in the cold.

'All aboard!' the train conductor called. The crowd of people grabbed their luggage and boarded, squeezing through the doors like oily shadows. Catherine pushed her face to the cold glass, trying to get a better view. The train seemed to go on forever from that perspective. She idly wondered if the train had no end, just carriages after carriages riding along an infinite track.

The train began moving again. She stared blankly outside as concrete buildings were replaced by larger longer slabs of concrete. She caught a brief glimpse of her reflection in the glass. Her hair was a mess. She had lost one of the bright red ribbons her mother had given her, causing her brown hair to hang loose at one side. The other side was ragged, no longer tied in a bow. She couldn't be bothered to try and fix it.

'Excuse me… Could I sit here?' Catherine turned to see a young man gesturing to the empty chair. He was wearing a coat much too big for him. She looked around; all the other seats were occupied.

'Fine,' she consented. He nodded in thanks and sat down.

For a while they both sat in silence, and Catherine continued to stare out of the window, bored. The city was becoming smaller and smaller, till all she could see was a mass of tiny street lights in the distance.

'They're beautiful.' Catherine turned. The man was also staring out of the window, his eyes glistening. Catherine cocked her head slightly.

'What are?' she asked, wondering what on earth he was blathering on about.

'The street lights – don't you agree?'

'It's just some street lights,' she said, confused. Catherine couldn't see what was so special about them.

'They remind me of stars,' he replied wistfully.

'I don't see why you're getting so excited; it'll be darker later so you'll see loads of stars then!'

'That doesn't stop this from being any less stunning,' he replied.

Catherine gazed at him a while before noticing something rather odd.

'Umm… mister, why are you wearing pyjamas?' she asked. Sure enough, the man was dressed in a pair of blue pinstriped pyjamas.

'Why do you look like you were dragged backwards through a bush?' he retorted. Catherine frowned and turned back to the window. The man sighed.

'I'm sorry. If you really must know, I came here from a hospital.'

'A hospital?' a female voice said suddenly from the seat behind. 'You must be a rich man.' The voice had a heavy accent to it. Both Catherine and the man turned around to find where the voice had come from. The woman sitting behind them had a pinched face with hollowed out cheeks; in coarse dry hands she gripped her train ticket.

'No, I'm not rich, just ill,' the man said, smiling.

'My son is very sick,' the woman said, looking forlorn. 'He coughs all through the night and can barely speak. There is a medicine that might save him but I could not afford it. I took another job to save up the money, but it was never enough. My son gets weaker and weaker every day. In desperation I took more and more work, only eating enough to carry on... But exhaustion caught up with me, and now my son will have no medicine.' When she finished her story she looked sadly at the man and then at Catherine, and said, 'I do not think it will be long till I see him once more.' Then the sad, strange woman got up and left the compartment.

Catherine turned to the man.

'I never realised there were people like that,' she said, sinking back into her seat.

'I know,' the man said in reply. 'She sacrificed so much to save what she loved.'

The train carried on regardless, and soon the man had fallen asleep next to Catherine. She thought about what the woman had said. Why was the world like that? It was so unfair! That lady had worked so hard and had got nothing in return! Why was the world this way? She sighed; it wasn't like she could do anything about it, not anymore. A star flashed past the train window. Catherine shook her companion awake – there was no way he would want to miss this!

'Look!' she said, pointing excitedly 'I told you there would be stars!' His eyes widened in amazement.

'It's almost as if I could touch them,' he gasped as they passed a vast constellation shining against the darkness of space. A pair of shooting stars blazed past, heading towards a small blue and green sphere in the distance.

'My mum told me once that shooting stars that fell together were reborn on earth as twins,' Catherine said, smiling at the memory.

'I rather like that,' the man murmured, as the train passed a rainbow-hued galaxy.

The man looked down at the ticket in his hands.

'I'm supposed to be having an operation, but even if I live I'll just be living on borrowed time,' he told her.

Upon hearing this Catherine frowned slightly.

'I think borrowed time is better than none at all,' she told him matter-of-factly, before noticing something: the train was going towards a tunnel.

'Last stop coming up!' the conductor called.

'Even so…What would be the point?' The man asked in reply to Catherine's previous statement. 'The world I'd be going back to isn't that wonderful.'

'But that could change… Don't you think?'

'What do you know about this? You're just a child!'

'Yeah, and I always will be. But the world won't fix itself – people need to do that bit.' Then she continued. 'If I could go home I would… but I can't. You, on the other hand – you can.' The man stared at her in confusion as the ticket collector made his way down the compartment. The man had to make his choice. Catherine wondered what thoughts were going through his head; regardless, she got her own ticket ready. The ticket collector was approaching fast. The man gave a brief look out the window, taking in the stars, before a determined look entered his eyes. He stood up, turning to smile at Catherine.

'Thank you,' he told her in a sincere tone. 'I hope we meet again someday.' Then he left the compartment.

'Tickets, please,' a voice intoned. Catherine looked up at the ticket collector, his face hidden in shadow. Catherine nodded and showed her slip of paper. The collector took it and carried on down the compartment.

She pulled open the window and stuck out her head, staring out at the stars. Then she heard a yell over the exhausted huff of the train. She turned to see standing on the tracks, dressed in pinstriped pyjamas, the man!

'My name's Dmitri, by the way!' he shouted, waving at her. She couldn't quite see his face but she was sure he was smiling.

She took a breath and from the bottom of her lungs yelled,

'I'm Catherine!'

The man turned and began to run down the tracks. Catherine was still staring when he was nothing but a pinpoint on the horizon, and the train entered the tunnel. Who knew what would happen from this point?

Lydia Shackleton

AquaraGym

Fish on treadmills, run like mad
Sharks pulling weights, building up their fins
Turtles on bike machines, spin, spin, spin

The fish run marathons, just like that
The sharks lift ten tonnes and get six-packs
The turtles cycle for hours, puff and pant

Then the fish fade away like clouds of steam
The sharks leave my sight, looking fit and lean
The turtles cycle out of view, damp from sweat
On my first visit to the AquaraGym

Sometimes I Write

Sometimes I write
a poem about
whatever I want

Sometimes I write
a poem about
whatever I want

Sometimes I write
a poem about
whatever I want

Sometimes I write
a poem about
whatever I want

Sometimes I write
a poem about
whatever I want

Sometimes I write
a poem about
whatever I want

And sometimes I don't

The Shortest Story

I'm unofficially an author.
I write unofficial works that are unofficially read
by unofficial people.
I go to unofficial signings
and unofficially sign
my unofficial works
for unofficial fans
with my unofficial signature.
And it's all done very
officially.

The Bear

One upon a time
There was a bear
He liked to scare
So I'll leave this story
Leave it there

Ghost Writer

I'm a ghost writer
I write for ghosts
I'm a ghost writer
I write for others, they say
I'm a ghost writer
Ghosts read my books
I'm a ghost writer
It isn't how it looks

Autumn

The leaves fall from the trees
Blackberries swell on branches
Migrating birds fill the skies
And the grass becomes pale brown

The leaves shrivel and die
Apples become crisp and juicy
Blackbirds roost in trees
And the grass becomes pale brown

The leaves become orange and gold
Red berries fill the bushes
Swallows dip for insects
And the grass becomes pale brown

The leaves carpet the ground
Pears become a multitude
Barn owls hoot at night
And the grass becomes pale brown

And all of this; this is all autumn

Ismaeel Shah

Beware, Beware

The monster lies silently under my bed. He is waiting, lurking around my room in the night, hovering over me like a demon. I am frightened to even take a peek. My heart is racing a thousand miles an hour as if it is in a drag race. *Thud...Thud...Thud.* He's churning up a plan. A plan to take me into his dimension with him. I can smell him; he smells like rotting food, rotten eggs. His claws cling against my floor. I feel slime on my face dripping onto the floor. *Drip... Drip... Drip.* I open my eyes and rush to the light to turn it on and look around the room. Under my bed, in the wardrobe, behind the curtains, but... nothing.

I lie back down, relieved, and fall back to sleep.

But next morning, I look on the floor and see a note of ebony black. Inside, it reads: 'Beware, beware, I am going to take you here,' above a picture of what looks like Hell...

Rooftop

On the rooftop
I stand
I stand
Looking for you
I stand
I stand
Trying to find you
I stand
I stand
until the roof falls through
I fall
I fall
Fix the roof with D.I.Y
I stand
I stand
on the rooftop
Looking for you

Morning

I woke up from my bed, not hearing the alarm clock go off or my mum yelling my name like usual. I looked at my watch to see the time, but it didn't work – and I'd only put new batteries in yesterday. 'Oh no!' I thought. 'School! I'm going to be late.' I leapt out of bed and stared out of the window, but I could hear no birds chirping and there were no people in sight. I walked down to find no one in the kitchen and no breakfast to eat. Where was everyone? Then I walked into the living room to find my mum frozen solid, stiff.

Tongue Twister

Tic tack trick tracks
Tracks trick tack tic

Matthew Ward

I Am Matthew

I know how the moon got its craters
How the stars got their shine

I know why older siblings are annoying
Why clowns are so funny but scary as well

I have been inside a volcano
I have seen lava bubble and rise

I have been a rocket ship blasting off into air
I have been a tree growing bigger and bigger
I have been a soldier fighting for my life
heard stone bombs hitting the ground hard

One day I will float in the sky

One day I will be sucked into a black hole
Sucked away from life

The Ukulele

I once had a tall grand neck like a giraffe,
a big fat body like a huge hippo,
until the operation.
I only went for a change of strings
but they shrunk my neck,
chopped up my big fat body,
ripped out my voice box,
changed it to a high-pitched squeal like a pig.
I cried for many weeks,
unable to play my song –
but now I sit on the hot beach of Hawaii
being played sweetly
by girls in grass skirt dresses
and they call me
Ukulele.

North and South

where you from?
Bradford, you?
London
oh, watch out
watch out for what?
people who hate Londoners
what do you mean? Why would people hate Londoners?
some Londoners are idiots
well, some Northeners are idiots
who you calling an idiot? Poshy.
Poshy, who are you calling Poshy, you little scratter
little scratter?! Who are are you calling scratter, you posey posho
scratter
posho
scratter

The Strange Man

I always see him: the strange man. He walks slowly past my house. I see him from my bedroom window. I can't see his face – he's always got his buffy collar up on his black leather coat, and a black hat on with a feather sticking out like a knife.

When I see him I look away in fright. One day I tried not to look away and I saw him approach the apple tree in our front garden. I've known that tree for years, since it was a sprout.

He looked at it in a strange way. He was staring at the biggest apple on the tree and licking his lips. He reached out his hand to grab it, but there was a policeman walking up the street, and he shouted, 'Oi! Get away from that tree, that's private property.'

The strange man heard him but carried on. He pulled the apple from the tree and chewed on it as he stared at the policeman. 'Right, I am arresting you for illegal apple picking.' But the man just stood still, eating his way through the apple and staring at the officer. Then suddenly the officer's trousers began to glow, and in a flash his pants fell down and his face went bright red as the strange man turned and walked off.

Six Word Stories

Ismaeel Shah

The cat lives in my hat.
Books love to read about me.
I am as big as an eclipse.
Dogs go shopping with ginger cats.

Samiual Mahmood

Chickens cross roads while eating chicken.
The man was unknowingly right, not.
The butcher cut his meat, precisely.
In the tub, drowned in blood.
Hippos cause hiccups, crocodiles cause handbags.

Lydia Shackleton

I am seriously bad at simple mathematics.
The world ended, and very suddenly.
Somebody answered The Big Question. Who?
I watched daisies push up concrete.

Daniaal Mahmood

Injury, anger, desperation, rehabilitation, determination
and success.
Pilot crashed and landed in desert.
Hiccups travelled far and wide, silent.

Matthew Ward

Never found an answer, simple question
Someone ate the banana, but who?

Biographies

Samiual Mahmood

Just a normal boy living his life in the heart of Bradford.

At the age of 5, I made friends. They give me the inspiration to write. I base most of my stories on my holidays and family. All this imagination starts in a small study room in the corner of a small house. You never know where you are going to go when writing a story... there are endless possibilities.

Seren Robb

Seren Robb is 15 years old. She lives in Bradford but lived in Keighley before moving. She has two cats even though she is allergic. She enjoys reading, writing and drawing; her favourite book is *The Phantom Tollbooth*. As a young child she devoutly believed in the existence of fairies and is not quite sure if she has fully dismissed their existence.

Lydia Shackleton

Has always lived in Bradford. She can roll her tongue into interesting shapes and enjoys murder mysteries. Her best Christmas present was a guinea pig named Snowy, she is obsessed with multiples of nine, she is afraid of people, and her favourite animal is a guinea pig. Did she mention guinea pigs?

Ismaeel Shah

I am just a boy living a simple life in this strange and wonderful world. I love to write about anything that comes to my mind and write it from my own perspective. I get my ideas from friends, family and even foes. I lay down on the sofa staring up at the ceiling thinking how far I am going to get in life and what goals I am going to achieve.

Matthew Ward

Matthew was born on the 10th June; he once had an incident where he fell in the bathtub fully clothed. He likes football, video games and is a creative human beening.

'My life is an open book'.

Daniaal Mahmood

My name is Daniaal and I am 16 years old. I live in the city of Bradford. What I like is an endless list but to sum it up; my art, my passion for football, my education and my family are all things that are important to me in life. When I play football it is as though I'm in another world. When I create a masterpiece, all the colours come to life around me. My family drives me on to succeed in life. All that mixed up in one bowl, is then splurged onto a single white paper. My pen is all I need to write, my life is an inspiration that I can recreate into my own stories. Stories from other people and ancient books, inspired me to awaken the writer in me.

Mohammad Talha Ahmed

I am Talha.
I am beautiful and bronze
my body is skinny and my head is flat
I have been put in a box and mailed down the stairs
I like to shower
and keep myself clean
and have taught my cat
how to groom

Matthew Ward

Final Word

I hate the negative opinions that people say about Bradford. Bradford is great place to live, and we have things that other cities don't have. It's a brilliant place and I am proud.

Bill Bryson says, 'Bradford's role in life is to make every place else in the world look better in comparison,' but has he been to Saltaire or Ilkley? Has he been to festivals in City Park or to any Bradford City games? Has he been to the schools in Bradford? St John's, Bradford Academy, Dixons City Academy? Has he seen all the religious places in Bradford, all the multiculturalism, the museums, the Media Museum, the Industrial Museum? The restaurants, all the different foods, and how we are the curry capital of the UK? So, Bill Bryson: get lost. Bradford is a brilliant, wonderful place to be.